HORRiD HENRY
Meets the Queen

HORRID HENRY
Meets the Queen

Francesca Simon
Illustrated by Tony Ross

Orion
Children's Books

Horrid Henry Meets the Queen originally appeared in
Horrid Henry Meets the Queen first published in
Great Britain in 2004 by Orion Children's Books
This edition first published in Great Britain in 2012
by Orion Children's Books
a division of the Orion Publishing Group Ltd
Orion House
5 Upper Saint Martin's Lane
London WC2H 9EA
An Hachette UK Company

1 3 5 7 9 10 8 6 4 2

ISBN 978 1 4440 0551 6
Printed in China.

www.orionbooks.co.uk
www.horridhenry.co.uk

For Mary Clayton and Niall MacMonagle

Look out for . . .

There are many more **Horrid Henry** books
available. For a complete list visit
www.horridhenry.co.uk

or

www.orionbooks.co.uk

Contents

Chapter 1

Perfect Peter bowed to himself
in the mirror.

"Your Majesty," he said,
pretending to present a bouquet.

"Welcome to our school,
your Majesty.
My name is Peter, your Majesty.
Thank you, your Majesty.
Goodbye, your Majesty."

Slowly Perfect Peter retreated
backwards, bowing and smiling.

"Oh shut up," snarled Horrid Henry.
He glared at Peter.

If Peter said "Your Majesty" one
more time, he would, he would…
Horrid Henry wasn't sure what
he'd do, but it would be horrible.

The Queen was coming to
Henry's school!

The real live Queen!

The real live Queen, with her dogs
and jewels and crowns and castles
and beefeaters and knights and horses
and ladies-in-waiting, was coming to
see the Tudor wall they had built.

Yet for some reason Horrid Henry
had not been asked to give the
Queen a bouquet.
Instead, the head, Mrs Oddbod,
had chosen Peter.

Peter!

Why stupid smelly old ugly toad
Peter? It was so unfair.

Chapter 2

Just because Peter had more stars than anyone in the 'Good as Gold' book, was that any reason to choose *him*?

Henry should have been chosen.
He would do a much better job
than Peter. Besides, he wanted to ask
the Queen how many TVs she had.
Now he'd never get the chance.

"Your Majesty," said Peter, bowing.

"Your Majesty,"
mimicked Henry, curtseying.

Perfect Peter ignored him.
He'd been ignoring Henry a lot
ever since *he'd* been chosen to
meet the Queen.

Come to think of it, everyone had
been ignoring Henry.

"Isn't it thrilling?"
said Mum for the millionth time.

"Isn't it fantastic?"
said Dad for the billionth time.

"NO!"

Henry had said.

Chapter 3

Who'd want to hand some rotten flowers to a stupid queen anyhow?

Not Horrid Henry.

And he certainly didn't want
to have his picture in the paper,
and everyone making a fuss.

"Bow, bouquet, answer her question, walk away," muttered Perfect Peter. Then he paused. "Or is it bouquet, bow?"

Horrid Henry had had just about enough of Peter showing off.

"You're doing it all wrong,"
said Henry.

"No I'm not," said Peter.

"Yes you are," said Henry.
"You're supposed to hold the
bouquet up to her nose, so she can
have a sniff before you give it to her."

Perfect Peter paused.
"No I'm not," said Peter.

Horrid Henry shook his head sadly.
"I think we'd better practise,"
he said. "Pretend I'm the Queen."
He picked up Peter's shiny silver
crown, covered in fool's jewels,
and put it on his head.

Perfect Peter beamed. He'd been begging Henry to practise with him all morning. "Ask me a question the Queen would ask," said Peter.

Horrid Henry considered.
"Why are you so smelly, little boy?"
said the Queen, holding her nose.

"The Queen wouldn't ask *that*!"
gasped Perfect Peter.

"Yes she would," said Henry.

"Wouldn't."

"Would."

"And I'm not smelly!"

Horrid Henry waved his hand
in front of his face.

"Poo!" said the Queen. "Take this
smelly boy to the Tower."

"Stop it, Henry," said Peter.
"Ask me a real question,
like my name or what year I'm in."

"Why are you so ugly?"
said the Queen.

"MUM!" wailed Peter. "Henry called me ugly. And smelly."

"Don't be horrid, Henry!" shouted Mum.

Chapter 4

"Do you want me to practise with you or don't you?" hissed Henry.

"Practise," sniffed Peter.

"Well, go on then," said Henry.

Perfect Peter walked up to Henry and bowed.

"Wrong!" said Henry. "You don't bow to the Queen, you curtsey."

"Curtsey?" said Peter.
Mrs Oddbod hadn't said anything
about curtseying. "But I'm a boy."

"The law was changed," said Henry.
"Everyone curtseys now."

Peter hesitated.
"Are you sure?" asked Peter.

"Yes," said Henry. "And when you meet the Queen, you put your thumb on your nose and wriggle your fingers. Like this."

Horrid Henry cocked a snook.

Perfect Peter gasped.
Mrs Oddbod hadn't said anything
about thumbs on noses.

"But that's ... rude,"
said Perfect Peter.

"Not to the Queen," said Horrid
Henry. "You can't just say 'hi'
to the Queen like she's a person.
She's the Queen. There are special
rules. If you get it wrong she can
chop off your head."

Chop off his head!

Mrs Oddbod hadn't said anything
about chopping off heads.

"That's not true," said Peter.

"Yes it is," said Henry.

"Isn't!"

Horrid Henry sighed.
"If you get it wrong, you'll be locked up in the Tower," he said. "It's high treason to greet the Queen the wrong way. Everyone knows that."

Perfect Peter paused. Mrs Oddbod
hadn't said anything about being
locked up in the Tower.

"I don't believe you, Henry,"
said Peter.

Henry shrugged.
"OK. Just don't blame me when you
get your head chopped off."

Come to think of it, thought Peter,
there was a lot of head-chopping
when people met kings and queens.
But surely that was just in the
olden days…

"MUM!" screamed Peter.

Mum ran into the room.

"Henry said I had to curtsey
to the Queen," wailed Peter.
"And that I'd get my head chopped
off if I got it wrong."

Mum glared at Henry.
"How *could* you be so horrid, Henry?
said Mum. "Go to your room!"

"Fine!" screeched Horrid Henry.

"I'll practise with you, Peter,"
said Mum.

"Bow, bouquet, answer her question,
walk away," said Peter, beaming.

Chapter 5

The great day arrived.
The entire school lined up in the
playground, waiting for the Queen.

Perfect Peter, dressed in his best
party clothes, stood with Mrs
Oddbod by the gate.
A large black car pulled up
in front of the school.

"There she is!" shrieked the children.

Horrid Henry was furious.
Miss Battle-Axe had made him stand
in the very last row, as far away from
the Queen as he could be.

How on earth could he find out
if she had 300 TVs standing way
back here?

Anyone would think Miss Battle-Axe
wanted to keep him away from the
Queen on purpose, thought Henry,
scowling.

Perfect Peter waited, clutching an enormous bouquet of flowers. His big moment was here.

"Bow, bouquet, answer her question, walk away. Bow, bouquet, answer her question, walk away," mumbled Peter.

"Don't worry, Peter, you'll be perfect," whispered Mrs Oddbod, urging him forward.

Horrid Henry pushed and shoved
to get a closer view.

Yes, there was his stupid brother,
looking like a worm.

Perfect Peter walked slowly
towards the Queen.
"Bow, bouquet, answer her question,
walk away," he mumbled.

Suddenly that didn't sound right.
Was it bow, bouquet?
Or bouquet, bow?

The Queen looked down at Peter.

Peter looked up at the Queen.

"Your Majesty," he said.
Now what was he supposed
to do next?

Chapter 6

Peter's heart began to pound.
His mind was blank.

Peter bowed.
The bouquet smacked him
in the face.

"Owww!" yelped Peter.

What had he practised?
Ah yes, now he remembered!
Peter curtseyed.
Then he cocked a snook.

Mrs Oddbod gasped.

Oh no, what had he done wrong?

Aaarrgh, the bouquet!
It was still in his hand.
Quickly Peter thrust it at the Queen.

Smack!

The flowers hit her in the face.

"How lovely," said the Queen.

"Waaaa!" wailed Peter.
"Don't chop off my head!"

There was a very long silence.
Henry saw his chance.

"How many TVs have you got?"
shouted Horrid Henry.

The Queen did not seem
to have heard.

"Come along everyone, to the
display of Tudor daub-making,"
said Mrs Oddbod.
She looked a little pale.

"I said," shouted Henry.
"How many…"

A long, bony arm yanked him away.

"Be quiet, Henry,"
hissed Miss Battle-Axe.
"Go to the back playground like
we practised. I don't want to hear
another word out of you."

Horrid Henry trudged off to the
vat of daub with Miss Battle-Axe's
beady eyes watching his every step.
It was so unfair!

When everyone was in their assigned place, Mrs Oddbod spoke. "Your Majesty, mums and dads, boys and girls, the Tudors used mud and straw to make daub for their walls. Miss Battle-Axe's class will now show you how."

She nodded to the children standing in the vat. The school recorder band played *Greensleeves*.

Henry's class began to stomp in the vat of mud and straw.

"How lovely," said the Queen.

Horrid Henry stomped where he'd been placed between Jazzy Jim and Aerobic Al.

There was a whole vat of stomping children blocking him from the Queen, who was seated in the front row between Miss Battle-Axe and Mrs Oddbod.

If only he could get closer to the
Queen. Then he could find out
about those TVs! Henry noticed a
tiny space between Brainy Brian
and Gorgeous Gurinder.
Henry stomped his way through it.

"Hey!" said Brian.

"Oww!" said Gurinder.
"That was my foot!"

Henry ignored them.

Chapter 7

Stomp.
Stomp.
Stomp.

Henry pounded past
Greedy Graham and Weepy William.

"Oy!" said Graham. "Stop pushing."

"Waaaaaa!" wept Weepy William.

Halfway to the front!
Henry pushed past Anxious Andrew
and Clever Clare.

"Hellllppp!"
squeaked Andrew, falling over.

"Watch out, Henry," snapped Clare.

Almost there!
Just Moody Margaret and Jolly Josh
stood in his way.

Margaret stomped.

Josh stomped.

Henry trampled through the daub
till he stood right behind Margaret.

Squish.

Squash.

Squish.

Squash.

"Stop stomping on my bit," hissed Moody Margaret.

"Stop stomping on my bit," said Horrid Henry.

"I was here first," said Margaret.

"No you weren't," said Henry. "Now get out of my way."

"Make me," said Moody Margaret.

Henry stomped harder.

Squelch! Squelch! Squelch!

Margaret stomped harder.

Stomp! Stomp! Stomp!

Rude Ralph pushed forward.
So did Dizzy Dave.

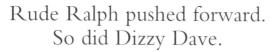

Stomp!

Stomp!

Stomp!

Sour Susan pushed forward.
So did Kung-Fu Kate.

Stomp!

Stomp!

Stomp!

Stomp!

Stomp!

A tidal wave of mud and straw
flew out of the vat.

 # Splat!

Miss Battle-Axe was covered.

Splat!

Mrs Oddbod was covered.

Splat!

The Queen was covered.

"Oops," said Horrid Henry.

Mrs Oddbod fainted.

"How lovely,"
mumbled the Queen.

HORRID HENRY BOOKS

Horrid Henry
Horrid Henry and the Secret Club
Horrid Henry Tricks the Tooth Fairy
Horrid Henry's Nits
Horrid Henry Gets Rich Quick
Horrid Henry's Haunted House
Horrid Henry and the Mummy's Curse
Horrid Henry's Revenge
Horrid Henry and the Bogey Babysitter
Horrid Henry's Stinkbomb
Horrid Henry's Underpants
Horrid Henry Meets the Queen
Horrid Henry and the Mega-Mean Time Machine
Horrid Henry and the Football Fiend
Horrid Henry's Christmas Cracker
Horrid Henry and the Abominable Snowman
Horrid Henry Robs the Bank
Horrid Henry Wakes The Dead
Horrid Henry Rocks
Horrid Henry and the Zombie Vampire

Colour books
Horrid Henry's Big Bad Book
Horrid Henry's Wicked Ways
Horrid Henry's Evil Enemies
Horrid Henry Rules the World
Horrid Henry's House of Horrors
Horrid Henry's Dreadful Deeds
Horrid Henry Shows Who's Boss

HORRID HENRY'S
Rainy Day

It's raining and Horrid Henry is
fed up. Until he decides to write
his will. But why should Henry be the
only one giving away his treasures?
It's much more fun getting stuff from
other people . . .

HORRiD HENRY'S
Author Visit

Horrid Henry's favourite author
in the whole world, TJ Fizz, is coming
into school. So when Miss Battle-Axe
sends him out of the class in disgrace,
Henry knows he just HAS to get back
– but how?